Pear Under the Stairs

First published 2010
Evans Brothers Limited
2A Portman Mansions
Chiltern Street
London W1U 6NR

British Library Cataloguing in Publication Data

Moorcroft, Christine.
Pear under the stairs. -- (Twisters rhymers)
1. Children's stories. 2. Stories in rhyme.
I. Title II. Series
823.9'2-dc22

ISBN: 9780237542535

Printed in China.

Editors: Nicola Edwards and Bryony Jones
Design: D.R.Ink
Production: Jenny Mulvanny

Pear Under the Stairs

Christine Moorcroft and Lisa Williams

Clare Macnair
had a rare
pink
pear.

She didn't want to share
the pear,
so she hid it under
the stairs.

Then she heard a noise
somewhere.
She looked out
into the square.

A crowd was there
on the way to the fair.

"Have you a pear to spare?" called a man with green hair riding bareback on a mare.

What a scare!
It made Clare's hair
stand up in the air.

"Look!" she said.
"My pockets are bare.
There is no pear."

Then another, riding a bear,
stared at Clare and said,
"Don't you dare
hide that pear
under the stairs!"

He dashed onto the kerb
with a swoop and a swerve.
"Get off there!" called Clare.
"What a nerve!"

"This isn't fair.
You must learn to share.
We're coming in there
to get that pear!"

Clare stood on a chair and
shouted, "Do what you like.
I don't care.
You shall not have my pear."

The crowd stared.
Clare was not scared!

She slammed the door and
sped under the stairs.
What on earth was she doing
in there?

Out came Clare. She threw the core without a care. “There’s your share of the pear!”

Twisters Rhymers follow on from the success of the **Twisters** series. Twisters are gripping short stories from different genres, told in just 50 words, with an appealing choice of illustration styles and content. Why not try one?

Not-so-silly Sausage by Stella Gurney and Liz Million 978 0237 52875 1
Nick's Birthday by Jane Oliver and Silvia Raga 978 0237 52896 6
Out Went Sam by Nick Turpin and Barbara Nascimbeni 978 0237 52894 2
Yummy Scrummy by Paul Harrison and Belinda Worsley 978 0237 52876 8
Squelch! by Kay Woodward and Stefania Colnaghi 978 0237 52895 9
Sally Sails the Seas by Stella Gurney and Belinda Worsley 978 0237 52893 5
Billy on the Ball by Paul Harrison and Silvia Raga 978 0237 52926 0
Countdown by Kay Woodward and Ofra Amit 978 0237 52927 7
One Wet Welly by Gill Matthews and Belinda Worsley 978 0237 52928 4
Sand Dragon by Su Swallow and Silvia Raga 978 0237 52929 1
Cave-baby and the Mammoth by Vivian French and Lisa Williams 978 0237 52931 4
Albert Liked Ladders by Su Swallow and Tim Archbold 978 0237 52930 7
Molly is New by Nick Turpin and Silvia Raga 978 0237 53067 9
A Head Full of Stories by Su Swallow and Tim Archbold 978 0237 53069 3
Elephant Rides Again by Paul Harrison and Liz Million 978 0237 53073 0
Bird Watch by Su Swallow and Simona Dimitri 978 0237 53071 6
Pip Likes Snow by Lynne Rickards and Belinda Worsley 978 0237 53075 4
How to Build a House by Nick Turpin and Barbara Nascimbeni 978 0237 53065 5
Hattie the Dancing Hippo by Jillian Powell and Emma Dodson 978 0237 53335 9
Mary Had a Dinosaur by Eileen Browne and Ruth Rivers 978 0237 53337 3
When I Was a Baby by Madeline Goodey and Amy Brown 978 0237 53334 2
Will's Boomerang by Stella Gurney and Stefania Colnaghi 978 0237 53336 6
Birthday Boy by Dereen Taylor and Ruth Rivers 978 0237 53469 1
Mr Bickle and the Ghost by Stella Gurney and Silvia Raga 978 0237 53465 3
Noisy Books by Paul Harrison and Fabiano Fiorin 978 0237 53467 7
Undersea Adventure by Paul Harrison and Barbara Nascimbeni 978 0237 53463 9